*To Roy, for help and sympathy
when the computer goes wrong!*
~ C F

*To Mom, Dad, Rach, Tim, Ange
and the rest of the back-up!*
~ L H

Copyright © 2005 by Good Books, Intercourse, PA 17534
International Standard Book Number: 1-56148-472-5

Library of Congress Catalog Card Number: 2004019531

Text copyright © Claire Freedman 2005 • Illustrations copyright © Louise Ho 2005.

Original edition published in English by Little Tiger Press,
an imprint of Magi Publications, London, England, 2005.

Printed in Singapore by Tien Wah Press Pte.

Library of Congress Cataloging-in-Publication Data

Freedman, Claire.
One magical morning / Claire Freedman; illustrated by Louise Ho.
p. cm.
Summary: Easy-to-read, rhyming text follows Mommy and Little Bear as they go out early one
morning to see the day dawn and find other woodland creatures awakening as they pass by.
ISBN 1-56148-472-5 (hard)
[1. Morning--Fiction. 2. Sun--Rising and setting--Fiction. 3. Mothers and sons--Fiction.
4. Bears--Fiction. 5. Forest animals--Fiction. 6. Stories in rhyme.] I. Ho, Louise, ill. II. Title.

PZ8.3.F88On 2005
[E]--dc22
2004019531

# One Magical Morning

Claire Freedman
Louise Ho

Good Books

Intercourse, PA 17534
800/762-7171
www.goodbks.com

In the shadowy woods,
one clear summer's morning,
Mommy took Little Bear
to see the day dawning.

The bears walked together
through grass drenched with dew.
Little Bear skipped,
as little bears do.

Little Bear gazed
as the sunrise unfurled.
"Up here," he cried,
"you can see the whole world!"

As the silvery moon
faded high in the sky,
Twinkle-eyed voles
came scurrying by.

And a little mouse gazed
as the morning sun
Melted the stars away,
one by one.

Fox cubs played while
the mist swirled like smoke,
Wrapping the trees
in its wispy cloak.

A pigeon coo-cooed
from a branch way up high.
Little Bear laughed,
"Look at me! Watch me fly!"

They stopped for a drink
at a babbling stream,
And the sun turned the forest
soft pink, gold and green.

Bushy-tailed squirrels
scampered down trees,
Hunting for pine cones
hidden by leaves.

"Look, Mommy!" cried
Little Bear in delight,
As a mole burst, blinking,
into the light.

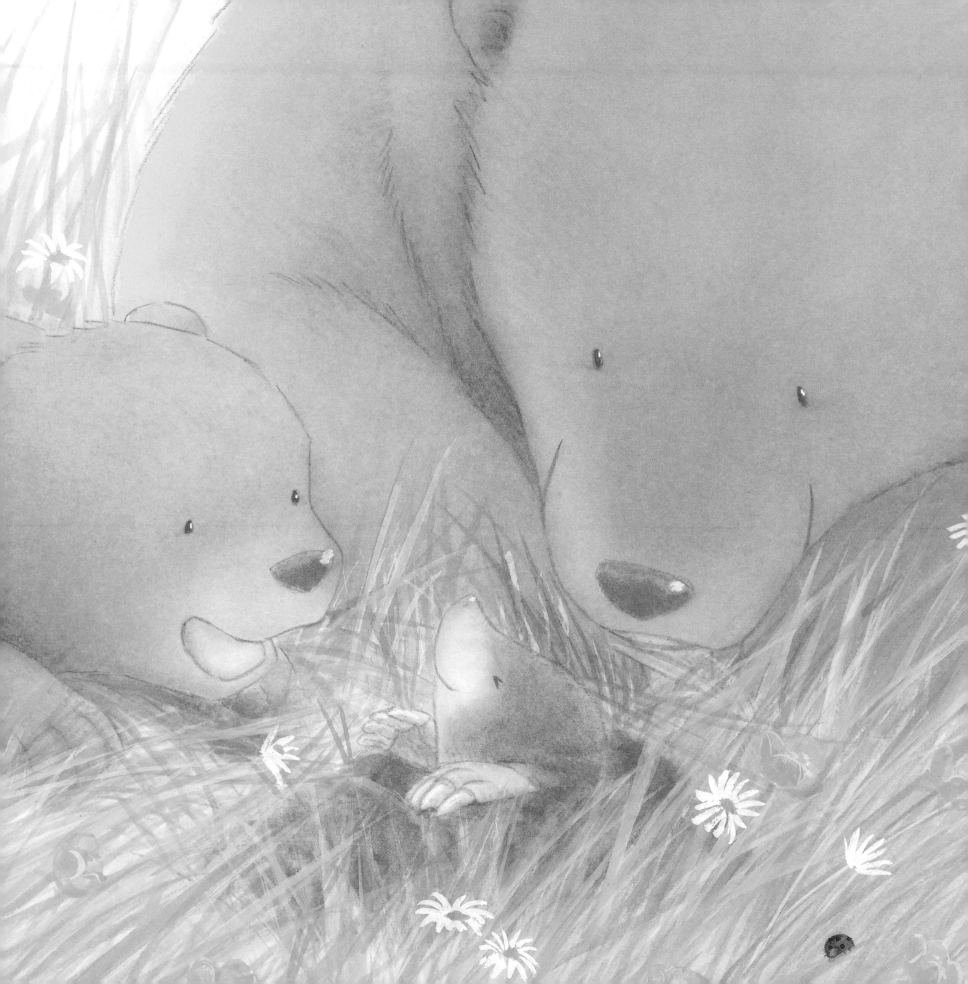

Mommy Bear smiled,
"Over here, take a peep!"
Bear's friend, Little Rabbit,
lay curled up asleep.

"Wake up, Little Rabbit,
come and play in the sun.
It's a beautiful day –
and it's just begun!"